MARTIAN
INVASION

Tales of a Terrarian Warrior, Book Four

MARTIAN INVASION

AN UNOFFICIAL TERRARIAN WARRIOR NOVEL

WINTER MORGAN

Sky Pony Press
New York

Sky Pony Press books may be purchased in bulk at special discounts for sales promotion, corporate gifts, fund-raising, or educational purposes. Special editions can also be created to specifications. For details, contact the Special Sales Department, Sky Pony Press, 307 West 36th Street, 11th Floor, New York, NY 10018 or info@skyhorsepublishing.com.

Sky Pony® is a registered trademark of Skyhorse Publishing, Inc.®, a Delaware corporation.

Visit our website at www.skyponypress.com.

10 9 8 7 6 5 4 3 2 1

Library of Congress Cataloging-in-Publication Data is available on file.

Cover design by Brian Peterson
Cover illustration by Amanda Bracken

Print ISBN: 978-1-5107-2196-8
Ebook ISBN: 978-1-5107-2198-2

Printed in Canada

TABLE OF CONTENTS

Chapter 1:
GONE FISHING

Miles woke up early, excited to get a jump on the day. He grabbed a quick breakfast, his new fishing rod and some bait, and stepped outside. The village was quiet as his friends slept soundly in their homes. Soon, he knew, it would be a bustle of activity, but unlike in the past when battles were on everyone's minds, the activity would all be peaceful fun and games.

Each night before bed, Miles read stories about legendary warriors and the great battles they fought. His dreams about mobs and drops, fighting techniques and quests, were all the adventure he needed now. Miles was glad his days as a warrior were over. Sure, he still had dreams of defeating Skeletron Prime. And the other day he had woken up certain he had been sleeping in a cave on his way to fight The Destroyer. But he always woke up in his bed, content knowing that The

1

Destroyer was banished, The Twins were defeated, and his warrior friends Owen and Asher were the ones constantly seeking out danger and taking on quests. Passing the torch to them so that he could live a quiet life in the village was a smart choice. Miles was certain of it.

Miles swung his fishing rod over his shoulder and whistled as he walked toward the ocean. It was only a few miles, and he enjoyed the brisk, early morning walk, watching the butterflies dance and admiring the flowers along the way. He couldn't believe that once he had walked these paths, questing for achievements, and had completely missed all the quiet beauty around him.

Just then, he heard a rustle in the bushes next to him. He instinctively reached for his sword, drew his weapon, and pointed it at the small, defenseless rabbit that had hopped onto the path in front of him. The rabbit stared blankly at Miles and hopped away, leaving Miles standing foolishly pointing his fishing rod at an empty space.

Miles laughed and placed his rod back over his shoulder, realizing he wasn't even armed. It was a good thing it was just a rabbit. Miles had gotten out of the habit of carrying even a small weapon when he left the village. A fishing rod wouldn't have done much damage to a hostile mob charge.

Before long, Miles reached the ocean. He breathed the fresh salty air and scanned the beach for a good place to start fishing. Not far down the sand, he spied an unusual item on the beach. It looked like something had washed up on the shore. Curious, Miles walked closer to investigate. As he peered over the mound, he gasped in surprise. It was a boy, and he wasn't moving!

Miles shook the boy gently and called out. "Hey, kid! Wake up! Are you okay?"

The boy opened his eyes and appeared to be dazed at first. He looked around as if to check his surroundings, then blinked at Miles. "Thanks for waking me up. I think I've been asleep for days!"

Miles helped the boy to his feet and tried to brush the sand off of his legs. The boy batted his hands away. "I can do that all by myself. I'm a big kid, after all."

Miles held his hands up and took a step back. "Of course you can. I was just trying to help. So what are you doing out here all alone?"

"I'm an angler. My name is Danny," the boy explained. "I could use your help, after all, actually. I may have a few jobs for you, if you're up for it."

Miles eyed him suspiciously. "What kind of jobs?"

"Oh, you know, the usual. I give you a daily fishing quest; you find me rare cool stuff; I give you a reward."

Miles considered Danny's offer. He had just gotten into fishing and loved the excitement of putting a baited hook into the water and coming up with something new and unexpected each time. "That sounds pretty cool, actually," Miles replied, sticking out his hand to shake Danny's. "I'm Miles, by the way."

Danny stuck out his closed hand to give Miles a fist bump, resulting in Miles accidentally shaking Danny's fist instead. He laughed awkwardly. "Paper covers rock, I guess."

Danny took his fist away angrily and held it behind his back. "No fair! I wasn't playing."

"I was just kidding," Miles apologized. "Hey, listen, what kinds of fish are you looking for?" he asked, quickly changing the subject.

Danny looked around to make sure no one was listening. He beckoned Miles to lean in closer and whispered, "A batfish!"

"A what?" Miles asked in surprise. He had caught a lot of fish since he started—and a lot of junk—but nothing that looked like a batfish.

"You find it underground, but no digging. That's the only clue I'll give you."

Ah, a puzzle. Miles liked puzzles. They were like the quests he used to go on as a warrior, but a lot less dangerous. "Underground but no digging, huh?" Miles thought for a moment, then he figured it out. "Like in a cave?"

Danny smiled and shrugged. "That's for me to know and you to find out."

Miles shook his head. Little kids could be so annoying. "There's a cave not far from here with a really deep fishing hole. I guess I'll start there." He looked over at Danny, but the angler wasn't giving any more cues. He started walking toward the cave and noticed Danny was following him.

The cave wasn't far away. As Miles entered, he looked back and saw Danny hesitate at the entrance. "It's safe, don't worry," Miles reassured him. "I've been here dozens of times and haven't seen anything worse than a spider or two."

Danny shrugged as if he didn't care, but he rushed to Miles's side and stuck close to him as Miles baited his hook and plopped it into the deep water. Almost instantly, Miles felt a tug at the line. He smirked at Danny as if to say that it was almost too easy, then reeled the line in. His smile instantly turned upside-down as he pulled up an old shoe. Danny snickered, but didn't say anything as Miles re-cast the line. His next haul was a tin can. Miles gritted his teeth, shifted to get more comfortable, and settled in for a long wait.

Fifteen bass, six tin cans, three speculars, two armored cavefish, and about three hundred shoes later, Miles was getting impatient. And hungry. He pulled out the snack he had packed for himself and looked over at Danny. Danny didn't say anything, but he didn't have to. The angler's stomach growled loudly at the sight of the food.

Miles wordlessly pushed half of his snack over to Danny. They munched quietly on their snacks as Miles put the last of his bait onto the hook and cast his line.

A quick tug told Miles he had a bite. He dropped his apple and reeled in carefully with both hands, knowing this was his last chance at succeeding at Danny's challenge. He wasn't sure why it felt so important. Danny hadn't even offered anything in return. But after living quietly for so long, a challenge, any challenge, stirred something in Miles that got him excited for a chance to prove himself.

He reeled in the last of the fishing line and a black fish appeared at the water's surface, flapping wildly. He didn't have to read the label to know it was a batfish—he could read it in Danny's triumphant expression. "You did it! You really did it!" Danny jumped around in his excitement, forgetting all about being afraid of the dark cave. "You're going to be really useful to me . . . I mean . . . we're going to be great partners, you and me."

"You and I," Miles corrected him as he handed over the fish. "Where do you live? It's getting late. I can walk you home."

Danny looked down and scuffed his feet in the dust. "Um, yeah, no biggie. I can go back to sleep by the water. Can you walk me there?"

"You don't have a house?" Miles asked. "What about a village?"

"You could build me a house . . ." Danny suggested eagerly. "Then I could send you on quests and give you challenges and we can explore together and go fishing and . . ."

Miles laughed. "I'm happy to build you a house. Come with me and I'll introduce you to my friends. You'll like them." Miles realized Danny had probably manipulated him into bringing him along, but he didn't mind. Having Danny around was almost like having a little brother and Miles was enjoying his company.

Danny started to follow Miles, then stopped and reached into his inventory. As Miles watched, he pulled out some high test fishing line, bait, and two gold coins, and handed them over. "This is yours. You earned it. For catching the fish. Okay?"

Miles placed the items carefully in his own inventory. "Thanks! Now let's get back to the village before it gets dark." Miles walked slowly, giving Danny a chance to keep up with his long strides. They took their time heading home, skipping rocks in a nearby pond and playing hide and seek.

It was mid-afternoon when they finally reached the village. He was surprised to find all of his friends crowded around two people, but he couldn't tell who they were. "Hello! I'm back from fishing! I caught an angler!" Miles picked Danny up and held him out as if he was a fish.

Danny giggled and squirmed free. "You didn't catch me. I caught you!"

Sarah the stylist was the first to reply. She broke free from the group and grabbed Miles in a giant hug. "You're back! Guess what? Look who's here and needs your help!"

The crowd of friends parted and Owen and Asher rushed toward Miles. Miles was startled to see them back in the village so soon. Last time he had seen them, they had agreed to part ways. "What are you guys doing here? I thought you were off fighting Plantera."

"We need your help," Owen said breathlessly.

"Thank goodness you're back!" Asher added. "We really need you this time."

"I'm sorry guys, but I'm not a warrior anymore," Miles replied apologetically. "Hard as it is to believe, I'm really happy living a quiet village life. I was just about to take on some new fishing quests for my new friend Danny, actually, as soon as I build him a new house."

"I have no place to go," Danny said with sad eyes. Miles could tell he was turning on the charm to try to win over Asher and Owen. "Mister Miles told me he'd make me a house and take care of me."

Bunny the party girl and Sarah took the bait, and started fawning all over Danny. "Oh, isn't he the cutest?" Bunny asked.

"You're the sweetest little thing!" Sarah said, rearranging his shirt and fixing his hair. "We'll take care of you, yes we will."

Owen put his arm around Miles. "Well, since the little guy is taken care of, now you're free to help us."

Asher did the same on his other side. "Let's get the Three Amigos together again! What do you say, old pal?"

Feeling trapped and a little confused, Miles didn't say a word. He didn't know what to say.

Chapter 2:
DON'T RAIN ON MY PARADE

With a backward glance at Danny to make sure he was in good hands, Miles reluctantly allowed himself to be led off by Owen and Asher to talk business.

"So first things first, how's quiet village life really treating you, Miles?" Owen asked with a knowing smirk. "It's pretty B-O-R-I-N-G, isnt' it?"

Miles shrugged. "Actually, it's pretty nice. I have plenty to do. I'm in charge of the whole village, and we have farms and this fishing thing, now . . ."

Asher interrupted him. "That's great, really great, but listen . . . We unleashed Plantera and he's kicking our behinds." He held out his arms, revealing rips in his clothing with cuts and bruises underneath. "We got shredded by the spike balls the first time. The second time, we got through that phase but got taken out by the hooks."

"It was really hard!" Owen agreed, showing Miles his own battle scars. "Then we dug a pit . . ."

"So you built an arena?" Miles asked, remembering all he had learned about the mob boss.

Asher and Owen looked at each other, clearly surprised. "You mean that's a thing?" Asher asked. "We just figured digging a hole could help with all the spiky balls bouncing around and those nasty seeds hitting us."

"Let me get this straight: you summoned one of the toughest bosses and didn't even have a game plan beforehand?" Miles was amazed. And disappointed. He had thought his friends were smarter than that. Why would he want to risk his inventory and health points and walk away from Danny's new challenges in order to help guys who didn't even know what an arena was?

"That's not how we roll, you know that, Miles," Asher said, laughing.

Owen joined in, laughing even harder. "Hey, Asher, you know how we roll, right?"

"DOWNHILL!" They both shouted together and collapsed into a fit of hysterical laughter. Miles just stared at them. He couldn't help feeling annoyed and left out. Clearly there was an inside joke that he was not a part of, and Miles felt like a third wheel, just like he had before they parted ways.

"Sorry, Miles, you had to be there," Asher said, recovering from his laughing fit. "We were running from a black scorpion and Owen tripped and fell on me, then I fell and we started rolling down this huge hill, and then . . ." Asher stopped suddenly. "I'm sorry, you're probably not interested in all the stuff we're doing. I get it. You've moved on."

"No, really, it's fine. It sounds like it was pretty funny." Miles forced a smile. He felt bad that he was annoyed. He was glad they were enjoying each other's company and part of him was a little jealous they were off having adventures together while he stayed home. "Look, I have stuff to do here, but I can give you some tips and help you make a plan for defeating Plantera if you want."

"That would be awesome!" Owen shouted. "What should we do? Tell me what weapons we need."

"Not so fast," Asher interrupted. "We don't just need your brain. We need your muscle too. You've got major battle skills, Miles. You're planting pretty gardens and going off on fishing trips . . . you might as well be an old wizard, sitting on a tree stump watching moss grow."

"He's got a point," said a familiar voice from behind him. Hope the steampunker stepped out of the shadows, tightening a bolt on her jetpack.

"You shouldn't eavesdrop," Miles said sullenly.

"Maybe not, but they are right," Hope replied. "You have great talent, Miles. You're wasting it here in the village. Don't pretend you don't miss the thrill of the battle."

Miles couldn't deny it. Just hearing about Asher and Owen and their epic fails in defeating Plantera got the wheels in his head moving. The stories he read weren't enough. He had lain awake many nights, thinking about how he'd set himself up to fight the giant poisonous plant, and he had his eye on the wasp gun drop he might get if he succeeded.

Asher took advantage of Miles's silence to press him further. "It'd only be for this one battle . . ."

"Unless you get a taste for spilling mob guts again, heh heh heh," Owen added.

Asher silenced Owen with a look, then turned back to Miles. "No, but seriously, just this one mob and we'll let you get back to fishing and whatever other cute little hobbies of yours that you have."

Miles looked from Asher to Owen, weighing his options. He could just say no and get on with building a house for Danny. But, he reasoned, that would be rude. They did come to him for help, after all.

He could give them some strategies and ask his friends in the village to help craft perfect weapons for their quest . . . a flamethrower, now that they'd defeated Skeletron . . . and a cobalt shield . . . Thinking of the glorious battle that awaited his friends, Miles unconsciously touched his hip where he usually kept his favorite sword. He came up with a handful of seeds. He had started wearing a seed pouch there for farming and feeding right after he hung up his weapons and armor. He flexed his fingers, realizing they were getting calloused from the farm chores and his muscles were aching from the hard farm work. He was in shape, and the call of the battle was strong.

Despite the awkwardness of traveling as a trio with Asher and Owen, they really did make a great team. Owen's skills were as strong as they were rough and untrained, and Asher was eager to learn. They needed a leader and, he realized, he needed them too.

"Okay," Miles said simply. "I'll do it." Asher and Owen jumped up to pat him on the back and thank him but Miles held up his hand to stop them in their tracks. "Hang on a second. I'll do it, BUT this is a one-time deal. I'm not going to follow up with a Lihzahrd Temple battle after we get the key, and I'm not going to take on any other challenges either."

"Fair enough, but what about stuff we encounter on the way? Are you going to leave us to fight zombies or mimics we run into?" Owen goaded him.

"We're not going to run into zombies because we're only going to travel in daylight, first of all," Miles replied impatiently. "And we won't find any mimics if we don't open any chests we find along the way, will we?"

"No, I guess not," Owen replied sullenly. "But what if we . . ."

"No. I'm coming to defeat Plantera and we're going in with a solid plan. You'll have to follow my lead and do what I say," Miles said sternly.

"Well, look who's turned into a boss mob of his own while we were away," Asher said snidely.

Miles glared at him and continued. "And when we're done, I'm going back to fishing and taking care of things here in the village."

Asher snorted in response. "Look, don't do us any favors. We thought you would be excited to leave all this behind and head out on the road with us again. But forget it. Whatever. We can do this without you."

Miles backed down. "I'm sorry, Asher. I didn't mean to be rude. I am excited. Really, I am. Thanks for asking me to join you."

Just then, they heard a gasp. They turned to see Katie the nurse rushing toward Owen and Asher with a look of angry concern on her face. "Oh no! What kind of trouble have you two been getting into lately? Come with me and I'll get you all fixed up."

"It's really not that bad," Asher protested as Katie pushed them toward her hut.

"I think it's pretty bad," Owen complained, holding his arm dramatically. "We lost a lot of health *and* I ripped my favorite shirt!"

"Come on in and we'll see what we can do about your cuts and scrapes. You'll have to speak with Sarah the stylist about your shirt, though," Katie said as she ushered them inside and closed the door.

Hope turned to Miles and put a hand on his arm supportively. "You're doing the right thing, you know."

"Am I?" Miles asked. "I hope you're right."

Chapter 3:
THORNY MESS

Miles knew Danny was in good hands with his friends in the village while he went off to help Asher and Owen. He promised the angler that as soon as he returned, he would build him the coolest house he had ever seen. Miles had been meaning to build a tree house like the one Isabella the dryad had shared with them in the Hallow. He would have loved a house like that when he was Danny's age. Actually, he'd love a house like that now.

To prepare for the battle with Plantera, Miles bought a stack of bombs from Jack the demolitionist, and packed up frost armor, along with an assortment of ranged and melee weapons to add to Owen and Asher's collection. At the last minute, he grabbed some trophies from the shelf before closing the door.

He met up with Asher and Owen, and they set off for the Underground Jungle. After they had

17

gone a few steps, Miles ran back to give his friends some last minute instructions. "Please be sure to take care of the garden while I'm gone," he said to Katie. "And the horse's saddle needs mending, if you don't mind, Cedric," he told the magician. Katie and Cedric nodded.

Sarah gave him a reassuring hug. "Don't worry, Miles. As much as you like to think you're in charge, we can handle things just fine without you."

Miles hugged her back. "It's a good thing I know how sarcastic you can be or I'd be offended!" he joked.

"Who said I was kidding?" Sarah replied with a wink and a smile.

Miles laughed and rejoined Asher and Owen who were waiting impatiently. "You really take this whole village leader thing seriously, don't you?" Asher asked.

Miles shrugged wordlessly. With his chores and responsibilities taken care of, he had already turned his thoughts to the battle ahead and was running through different game plans in his head to decide which one had the best chance of defeating Plantera.

Asher and Owen chatted excitedly as they walked, talking about what had gone wrong in their previous battles with the mob. Miles half-listened, nodding appreciatively, but mostly he was trying to recall everything he had learned about the mob: thorn balls, seeds, spores, tentacles and hooks, but he couldn't remember what order they came in. Were the poisonous spores first? Or the hooks? Maybe the seeds because they were the weakest . . . Miles was lost in thought and didn't see they had already gone underground to enter Plantera's domain.

Suddenly, a small pink seed smacked him in the head and plopped down on the ground next to him. "Oh, right. It's seeds first," he said out loud. Miles looked up and saw the large pink blossom inching toward them using long tentacles. It was bigger than he had expected. Miles quickly drew his sword and began to hack at the tentacle. "We have to retreat!" he shouted to his companions. "We need time to dig an arena and put our weapons in order."

"We have to deal some damage first to slow it down," Asher said. He shot arrows at the mob while Owen copied Miles and hacked at the tentacles with his own sword. Plantera took some damage but continued to advance. Satisfied they had made some progress, the three retreated above ground to plan their attack.

Miles checked his sword and armor and saw they hadn't taken too much damage. Owen had a small cut on his arm that looked like it would heal on its own, and Asher seemed completely fine. "Looks like we're all okay so far," Miles announced. "Let's get organized before heading back down there."

Owen nodded. "You're already a good leader. We never thought to get organized beforehand in any of our other battles." He looked accusingly at Asher, who just shrugged unapologetically.

Miles jumped in before they could start arguing. "Let's set up these heart statues just inside the cave," Miles said, pulling them from his inventory. "I was keeping them as trophies since I gave up fighting, but we can use them now. I'll activate them with these pressure plates I bought so we can top off our health as we go."

"Next, let's dig an arena. I think a big trench lined with wooden platforms will let us use our jetpacks to dodge Plantera's attack and shoot from the landings. Since there are three of us, this will be a lot easier," Miles continued, rattling off instructions. He explained how they could knock holes in the jungle walls and create recesses to hide in when Plantera released its hooks. Asher and Owen were listening wordlessly and Miles realized he had completely taken control of the situation. "So what do you guys think?" He asked, hoping he hadn't offended them with his bossiness. "What types of weapons did you bring?"

Asher pulled out a mushroom spear. Owen grinned and pulled out the Megashark they had used in their last adventures together. "Remember this? I picked up some Chlorophyte Bullets too."

Miles laughed and nodded. He couldn't forget the weapon that had helped him destroy the last mechanical boss he had faced. "Excellent choice, Owen," he said. "Hey, since you're the fastest, start out with your sword or anything you have to hit the seeds back at Plantera. You can use the Megashark later." Owen nodded. "Asher, use your sword to hack at the tentacles to keep them back." Miles continued. "I'm an experienced farmer, so I'll dig the trench." Miles was putting his complete trust in them while he was defenselessly digging the trench, but he knew they'd be there for him.

"We've got your back," Asher said as if he had read Miles's mind.

"Okay, everyone have their armor and weapons in order?" Miles asked, pulling out his shovel. "Let's go!" The three warriors marched fearlessly back into Plantera's lair.

As soon as they arrived, they were pelted by seeds, but this time they were ready. After the first stinging blow to his cheek, Owen used his broadsword to hit every seed that came his way. He had ninja-quick moves, Miles noticed as he shoveled more quickly than he had ever moved before. It was good, hard, mindless work. His senses were alert to the ping of the seeds against Owen's broadsword and the sounds of Asher's sword hacking away at Plantera's tentacles. "Take that!" Miles could hear Asher shouting happily, while Miles kept his head down and focused on the task of digging the widest, deepest trench he could.

"Miles, look out!" Owen shouted, but Miles didn't have time to duck. He was hit by a thorn ball. Before he could get any weaker, he ran over to the heart statue and collected a bunch of hearts as they popped out. Feeling refreshed, he jumped back into the pit and started putting up platforms, keeping an eye out for thorn balls and seeds. He watched as a nearby seed hit the ground and instantly sprouted. The jungle around him was growing. He knew they needed to move quickly. As he completed the arena, he set his mind on crafting a plan to end the spread of the seeds. They were growing like weeds.

"That's it!" he shouted. "We need a weed killer!"

"What?" Asher called out breathlessly. He was swatting away seeds like he was at a batting cage.

"I can use my flamethrower to knock out the seedlings," Miles called back. He pulled out the flamethrower he had crafted after battling Skeletron Prime and charged it to full power.

"Wait! Stop!" Owen called out. "It's not strong enough . . ." But it was too late. Miles pulled the trigger and released the flame across the growing field of sprouted Plantera seeds. It hit a few nearby sprouts, but fizzled out. Meanwhile, Miles was pelted with three more seeds.

"Ouch," Miles said softly, heading back to the heart statue to heal his wounds.

"If you think that hurts, wait 'till the spike balls start coming after you," Asher said. As if Plantera had heard him, a thorn ball bounced toward Asher. He shot up into the air using his jet pack to dodge the attack. "It looks like the fun has really started now!" he called happily.

Miles quickly put some wooden platforms in place and dodged three thorn balls in the same way as he built, shooting upward with his jet pack when the thorn balls came near. When he was satisfied with the arena, he called to Owen and Asher. "Looks like we're ready for whatever Plantera wants to throw at us!"

They topped off their health at the heart statue and began dodging balls as they flew toward the evil pink bulb. Plantera made its way into the arena, shooting out tentacles and moving toward each of them. Miles landed on a platform at close range, using his flamethrower to singe the bulb. Owen fired his Megashark from a landing slightly farther away. Asher stood at the top of the arena and held up his mushroom spear, shooting mushrooms that bounded toward Plantera. There seemed to be a rhythm to their battle—fly, land, shoot, dodge—and they found it easy to avoid the seeds and thorn balls since they had their jet packs.

When the mob's health reached 50 percent, the pink petals fell off to reveal a large green mouth. Without its petals to slow it down, Plantera sped up its attack. Miles found it hard to get into a new rhythm, and bumped into more than a few thorn balls as he tried to coordinate dodging and shooting. He couldn't fire while he was flying, but he couldn't dodge while he was on a platform. He glanced over and saw Owen was doing just as badly. Asher was standing at the top of the arena, hacking at hooks and batting away seeds as he dodged spores. He was clearly in top form, Miles noticed. His skills and his confidence had definitely improved since their last battle.

Just then, he felt a tug at his sleeve. Thinking it was Owen asking for help, he wheeled around. "What now?" he said impatiently, but it wasn't Owen. On Miles's shirt was a giant hook on a leash attached to Plantera's main bulb. Before he could respond, he was pulled off the platform and thrown at the ground. Pain shot through him as he felt the barbs pierce his skin, and he heard a crunch as he landed on the ground.

Afraid the sound was a broken bone, he lay still for a moment, checking his body for pain. Aside from a few cuts and bruises, he found he had just had the wind knocked out of him. He rolled over and discovered the crunch was actually his jetpack which had broken his fall.

Asher looked down at him. "You okay?"

"I'll be okay," Miles replied, feeling more embarrassed than hurt. He tried to get up but found he was still breathless from the fall. Luckily the heart statue wasn't far away. He crawled toward it, hoping Plantera wouldn't sense his presence and focus on him.

A tentacle suddenly shot toward him with a small, toothy bud at its end. "Watch out for biters!" Owen called out. Miles reached for his sword, but he wasn't strong enough to aim it. He closed his eyes and braced himself for the hit, hoping it wouldn't hurt too much.

Chapter 4:
THE KEY

Everything seemed to be moving in slow motion with his eyes closed. Miles could hear the chomping of the biter's teeth, and the sounds of battle above him. But instead of hearing a "CHOMP" and feeling the searing pain of a lethal bite, he heard a simple "plop." No pain. He opened one eye to see the bud lying on the ground next to an arrow. He looked up to see Owen smiling as he put away his bow. "You're welcome!" Owen laughed before turning back to face the hooks and seeds coming at him from above.

Miles managed a weak "Thanks," then continued inching toward the heart statue. Once he activated it and powered up his health, he was able to patch up his jet pack. It wasn't at full power, but he could use it to hop between platforms and dodge the thorn balls bouncing nearby. He hopped up on the platform next to Asher.

"What happened down there?" Owen asked. Miles could tell he was disappointed.

"I got hit by a hook," Miles said, embarrassed. "Kind of a noob move, huh?"

"You're just a little rusty, that's all," Owen replied with a shrug.

Then Asher appeared grinning at his other side. "Out of practice, are we?" he asked mockingly.

"A little, I guess." Miles blushed. He couldn't believe how dull his skills had gotten in the short time he had been "retired" from fighting. Battling used to be his life, and now he couldn't even dodge a stupid plant. He was so angry at himself. He whipped out his Crystal Storm and shot it at Plantera to vent his rage. The bulb shrank back in surprise and pain.

"Nice shot!" Asher said. "You've been holding out on us!"

"You just wanted to see what we could do on our own, right Miles?" Owen said, looking at him with admiration.

"Unfortunately, no. I'm just rusty." Miles said. "But that shot really felt good!" he said grinning. "I'm dusty, I'm sore, and I have more cuts than I can count, but yeah, I'm glad I came!"

Asher clapped him on the back happily. "We're glad you came too. Now let's finish this!" With a nod, they all whipped out their weapons and aimed them directly at Plantera. "All together now! One . . ."

"Two," Owen called.

"Three!" Miles replied. They unleashed the mushroom spear, Megashark, and flamethrower at once, reducing Plantera to a mess of pulp before it shriveled up and disappeared.

They broke into a cheer, hugging each other and laughing, "You may have lost your fighting edge, but we couldn't have done it without your knowledge and planning skills," Asher said to Miles.

"You guys have leveled up since our last battle together," Miles replied.

Owen retrieved the drops: a grenade launcher, a Rocket I, a Nettle Burst and a key. "What's this key for?" Owen asked.

Miles inspected it. "It's the key to an underground jungle temple. It's also called a Lihzahrd Temple," Miles recalled, glad he had been keeping up on his reading. "But as we agreed, I'm not going there with you. I'm going home."

"Where's your sense of adventure?" Asher asked. "You love exploring, and we don't even have to travel far . . ."

"And we can still be home in time for dinner." Owen added.

Miles backed down. Exploring was one of his new favorite hobbies. Besides, everyone back home was minding the village already. He could treat it as a little vacation, he reasoned. A few more hours couldn't hurt. Besides, they clearly needed his advice. Maybe he wouldn't fight . . . he'd just give them advice. "Anyone have an extra jet pack?" he asked.

"That's the spirit!" Asher said, digging into his inventory and handing Miles a brand new Jet Pack. "Hope gave it to me as a parting gift," he explained.

Miles mumbled his thanks and strapped it onto his back. He tried to remember what he had read about the legendary Cave Monster Battle of long ago. Fighting the Lihzahrd would earn them one Power Cell which would summon the Golem Boss. That was one boss he was definitely not willing to fight. Mostly because it sounded scary, but also because he hadn't gotten up to that chapter in his book, *Legendary Battles of Terraria*, and he didn't know the first thing about it. His knowledge had become his biggest asset to the team, and he didn't want to make Owen and Asher's fight even more difficult by protecting his dead weight in a fight. Well, he reasoned, he'd cross that argument when they got to it, but first they had to get to the temple, which had challenges of its own.

They left the arena, taking the heart statues with them for their next adventure, and traveled down to the underground jungle temple. "So, what do we need to know before we go down there?" Asher asked Miles.

"I've never been to a jungle temple, but it sounds like the traps are worse than the enemies." Miles told them how they need to avoid stepping on the pressure plates once they find them, and about the Lihzahrd mobs, who would come at them in a large pack but should be easy to take out.

"How will we know where the traps are?" Owen asked, sounding nervous.

"We'll send you in first and once you get hit, we'll know!" Asher laughed.

Owen's face turned an angry shade of red. "We tried that once and it all went horribly wrong!"

"I'm sorry. I was just kidding," Asher said. It seemed to Miles that the two of them were acting more like brothers than fellow travelers and he felt a pang of jealousy. "But seriously, how DO we trigger the traps to find them before they find us?"

"Unfortunately, Owen, Asher's plan is the only way I know how without summoning minions," Miles said. "But we don't need to send you in as bait. We're the Three Amigos, right? We'll walk in slowly . . . together." Owen looked at Asher who nodded in agreement.

"Thanks, guys," Owen sounded relieved. "Let's go. I feel ready!"

The moment they entered the first corridor, the floor creaked and a spiky ball bounded toward them. Miles jumped just in time to avoid the ball.

Owen spun around and hit the trap with an arrow on his first shot. "Easy peasy!"

Asher took the lead next, but a few steps in, Miles grabbed his arm to stop him. "Spike," he cautioned Asher, who walked carefully around the wooden spike in front of him. It was Miles who spotted the first Lihzahrds, marching toward them on two feet. Miles threw a bomb into the middle of the crowd and took out five at once. One of the mobs was thrown clear by the blast, landing on a pressure plate which shot a jet of fire through four more Lihzarhds. "Boo yah!" Miles shouted gleefully. "That's how it's done!"

Asher nudged Owen with a smile. "Think he's having fun now?" he asked playfully.

This isn't as bad as I thought it would be, Miles thought as he stepped forward confidently. Unfortunately, that step could have been his last. High speed poisonous darts shot out from either wall, straight at Miles. He ducked, letting one fly over his head, but moved into the line of fire of another dart. Pain seared through his side and he suddenly felt lightheaded and dizzy. Asher rushed toward him and he heard him speak as if he was. very far away. "Owen, take out those traps. I'll take care of Miles." Miles assumed Asher would catch him as he fell, but instead Asher grabbed his inventory and started rifling through it.

"So, that was your plan all along, huh?" Miles said with a weak laugh. "Lure me to the Lihzhard's Temple and steal my stuff?"

"Save your strength and quiet down while I set up this heart statue, will you?" Asher said gently.

Miles lay still and listened to the sounds of the temple. The ground hummed with an electric pulse and Miles felt the beat of it run through him. He bolted upright, ignoring the pain and nausea. "Electricity!" he shouted. "The traps are all wired. Use a wire cutter to find all the wires, then take out all the wires to stop the traps."

"That poison went to your head. Lie back," Asher scolded him. "I'm almost finished with this heart sculpture . . . There!" A heart bounded out and landed on Miles's chest. He instantly felt a little better. Three more hearts rained down on his head and legs and he was able to stand upright. Miles triggered the heart a few more times to restore his health while Asher shot at a handful of flying snakes with his Megashark. "Take that you slithery, slimy monsters!"

"Miles is right!" Owen shouted from far away. He had made it most of the way down the corridor. He reappeared holding up a wire cutter and a handful of wires. "That takes care of the traps from here to the next turn."

"Nice work disabling the traps!" Asher said with admiration. "Both of you. I knew you were worth bringing along," he added, looking at Miles. Miles winced, feeling like he had a long way to go before he felt truly useful.

Once they knew how to navigate the traps and the mobs, Miles had to admit that it was smooth sailing to get to the Lihzahrd Altar. Owen was happy to dart ahead now that the traps were gone, gleefully taking out the Lihzahrds and flying snakes. Suddenly, he shouted. Miles and Asher ran up to see what he found. "A chest! I found a chest! Can I open it?" He looked like a little kid who finds a present the day before his birthday. "Please?"

Miles stood in front of it. "Better not, Owen. It could be a trap." Miles had found more traps that were boobytrapped with mimics and worse in his explorations. He didn't want to admit that the poison darts had weakened him, but he really wasn't up for another fight so soon.

"What's wrong with you, Miles?" Owen said angrily. "You used to be fearless. You may be more book-smart now, but you're afraid of everything too."

Asher nodded in agreement. "When you stop second-guessing yourself, you increase the fun. You've said so yourself whenever we've doubted ourselves before. Besides, what's the worst that can happen? You get hurt and wake up at home in your own bed." Asher's words felt like a dare and Miles felt compelled to open the chest just to prove to himself and to the guys that he wasn't afraid. Miles had never been one to take a dare, but somehow whenever Asher challenged him, he always rose to the challenge. It drove him crazy, but it also made him feel good when he proved himself.

Then again, Miles thought, was it really worth it? Whatever was in that chest wasn't going to change his life a whole lot if it *was* a good thing, and if it was a bad thing . . . well, he'd had enough of bad things come his way in the past few hours. In fact, he had been bad-thing-free for days on end before these two showed up. "Leave it be, Owen. It's not worth it." Miles said, placing his hand firmly on the trunk. Miles breathed a satisfied sigh. He knew in his heart he had made the right decision.

Chapter 5:
IN THE TEMPLE

"Go ahead. Open it," Asher said.

"I wouldn't if I were you," Miles countered.

Owen looked from Miles to Asher and then down at the chest. "I'm doing it," he said with uncertainty, waiting for them to stop him. When no one made a move, Owen opened the chest. The other two stepped back cautiously. Owen smiled broadly and pulled out a Lihzhard power cell. "Ta daa!" They all breathed a sigh of relief. Asher looked coolly at Miles.

"What, no 'I told you so'?" Miles asked.

Asher shook his head. "You've been out of the game too long, man."

Miles didn't know how to respond, but he didn't have to. A horde of flying snakes flew at them from all directions. "Is it me, or do those snakes have tiny demon wings?" Miles observed, ducking under the cover of a nearby overhang.

"Definitely demon wings," Asher said, standing over a flying snake that had fallen to his sword. "Owen, make a barrier so we can go lower and keep the snakes out," Asher called to him, then turned to Miles. "Can you take some out, or are you too scared to fight now?"

In answer to his challenge, Miles whipped out his flamethrower and barbecued three snakes above his head, then grinned at Asher. "I'm good."

"Welcome back, brother," Asher said. They fought back to back and descended lower into the temple as Owen constructed a wall above their heads. Once they were sealed off, they had a little time to breathe a sigh of relief. Miles was able to plant the heart statue and activate it with a pressure plate, thanks to the wires Owen had collected. They had a quick snack and refreshed their health as they looked around the chamber. It was quiet. Too quiet, after all they had just been through.

"Where's the boss?" Owen whispered.

"The Golem?" Miles asked. "You have to activate it with the power cell you just picked up. I'll tell you how to defeat it if you want, but remember my promise—I'm not fighting any more hard bosses for you guys."

"Like you've been such a big help in battle already . . ." Asher said sarcastically. "Come on, Miles. You love this stuff. All kidding aside, we need you."

Miles looked at the altar, remembering all the hardmode bosses they had already fought. He suddenly felt like he was back at school and had just taken a test he had studied really hard for. The next day in school he'd come back to start an even harder unit, and all he'd see for the next nine months ahead is more studying and more tests. Only with hardmode bosses, you don't get a grade . . . bosses are pass/fail. Either you defeat the boss or you get sent back and have to do it all over again.

"No thanks," Miles said. "I really just want to go home. Just hide behind a barrier and shoot the head and avoid the missiles after level one," he added. "I haven't read the chapter on defeating the Golem yet, so I can't tell you anything you don't already know."

"Three heads are better than one," Owen said hopefully.

"Better than two, you mean," Asher corrected him. "And three sets of weapons are definitely better than two."

Miles shook his head and started climbing back up toward the exit. "I've failed you more than I've helped so far. You're the ones who were second-guessing yourselves thinking you needed me. The Three Amigos will be just fine as the Debonair Duo again. You guys will do great on your own."

Asher shook his head wordlessly. Owen looked disappointed. "Thanks for everything you've done.

We couldn't have gotten here without you, for what it's worth," Owen said as Miles mined through the barrier to leave them.

"Come find me and tell me all about it when you're done," Miles called back to them. "I'll have Bunny throw one heck of a victory party for you!"

Miles heard them place the power cell into the barrier and heard the Golem roar to life. He pulled himself up to the next level and was about to close the gap behind him when he heard a piercing scream and a cry for help.

Chapter 6:
STONE-HEADED GOLEM

Miles scrambled back down, quickly replacing the block that sealed out the flying snakes and Lihzhards. One Lihzhard got through and Miles quickly pierced it three times with his broadsword and grabbed its power cell drop before jumping down into the pit with his friends. The Golem was huge. Much bigger than Miles had imagined. The Golem was moving slowly, but because the room was small, it didn't need to be fast—it just had to be deadly. Fire balls shot from the Golem, along with large projectiles that looked heavy and harmful. Owen and Asher had their shields up, but they hadn't heeded his warning to put up a barrier they could shoot through.

"You guys never listen!" Miles called out as he quickly threw up a barrier between his friends and the Golem. "Now shoot through the wall . . ."

"Are you crazy?" Asher shouted. "We can't shoot through a wall. To do that we'd need a Vilethorn. Wait—do you have one?"

"No," Miles said impatiently grabbing Asher's inventory. "Use the Nettle Burst we picked up from Plantera. It's not just a trophy. It shoots through walls."

Asher's eyes opened wide. "No way! That's totally cool!" He grabbed the Nettle Burst and started shooting at the Golem's body.

Miles grabbed the weapon from him. "You seriously never listen to anything I tell you. Hit the head. Take out the head and you take out the Golem."

Asher grabbed the weapon back and aimed at the Golem's head, rapidly taking down the boss's health points. "What do we do?" Owen asked impatiently. "Just stand around doing nothing? Sounds like a Dynamic Solo, not a Duo or a bunch of Amigos."

"We protect the shooter," Miles replied. "And when Asher's Mana runs out, it's your turn to shoot. That's why we need three people, so we can build up Mana to run the magical weapons." Miles held up his shield in front of Asher to protect him from an incoming fireball that snuck through a hole in their defense. "Better patch up that hole, Owen."

"Yes, sir." Owen replied sarcastically, but he obediently placed a block to seal the hole.

The Golem's health points fell lower and Asher was almost gleeful as he continued to shoot until his Mana was almost empty. "We need a star statue . . . I'm almost out of Mana."

"Sorry, fresh out of statues," Miles replied. "But now Owen can have a turn." Miles took the Nettle Burst from Asher and handed it to Owen. "You're up!"

Suddenly, the Golem regained strength. It had entered the next phase and started shooting energy bolts at them. "Shields up!" Asher called out, raising two shields—one for himself and one for Owen.

Miles raised his own shield and realized the energy bolts were coming through the barrier. "The barrier isn't holding in this next stage, anyone have ideas?"

"Let's use our jetpacks to dodge the attacks while Owen holds him off with the Nettle Burst," Asher suggested, shooting up into the air and weaving to avoid the projectiles. Miles did the same, realizing they were drawing the Golem's fire away from Owen, making it easier for him to aim and shoot.

"Hey guys?" Owen called out. "My Mana is running low." Miles flew over to relieve him. "I don't think I did much damage," he said sadly.

Miles took the Nettle Burst from him and told him he did a great job. He weighed the Nettle Burst in his hand and was suddenly filled with confidence. A confidence he hadn't felt since he held the Pwnhammer in his hands after beating the Wall of

Flesh to enter hardmode. *I can do this*. He thought to himself. *I was born to do this*. He raised the Nettle Burst and with all his might shot it at the Golem's head with a rapid burst. The Golem shook from the blow. It shuddered, shot out three balls of fire, then collapsed as its head flew straight up to the ceiling and stuck there.

Asher flew in a victory lap, whooping with joy, thinking that was the end of the boss. Unfortunately, there was more to come. Now the Golem was smaller and more powerful, and they still had the head to deal with. Detached from the body, the Golem's giant head shot out lasers while its body shot fireballs. With attacks now coming from two locations, the trio was on even higher alert. "Shields up!" Miles called, reminding them to keep protecting themselves. "Owen and Asher, aim at the head. I'll keep at the rest of it!" Miles was on fire—not literally, of course—but he felt powerful and alert, even sensing when fireballs and spikes were rebounding off the walls behind him. He batted them away with Nettle Burst then resumed firing at the body to keep weakening the boss.

Owen and Asher met up at the heart statue to recover while Miles continued his amazing display of battle skills. "He's unstoppable," Owen observed.

Asher nodded. "He's always been this good, he just forgot how to fight for a minute. It's like riding a bicycle. You never forget once you learn."

"What's a bicycle?" Owen asked.

"Never mind," Asher said, shooting up to draw the Golem's fire away from Miles and aiming at the head with his Megashark.

"Hey guys?" Miles said. "I think my Mana is running out. Just a heads up."

"Whack it with everything you've got, Miles," Asher replied. "Pick a weapon and have at it!"

Miles threw a bomb, then grabbed his Palladium Repeater from his inventory. "This should do the trick." He fired a load of ammunition that rained down on the Golem for a full minute, rapidly bringing the Golem's health down to zero before it suddenly winked out of existence in a puff of smoke.

Quiet fell once again on the chamber as the three companions looked around in wonder. "Did we really do it?" Owen asked.

Asher flew off the cliff where he had been perched and circled the room with a loud Whoop. "Victory lap! We really did it!" he shouted.

"We really did it," Miles echoed quietly in disbelief.

They all met up at the statue to refresh their health and stared over at the altar. "Nice job, guys," Miles said. "You're really great warriors."

"We couldn't have done it without you," Owen said. "Right Asher?"

Asher nodded. "It's true. You and your plans keep saving the day."

Miles just shook his head. He was an extra body in the fight, that's all. Anyone with Mana could have manned that staff.

"Let's grab that altar and get out of here," Asher said, using a pickaxe to remove the altar. "I recall someone saying something about throwing us a celebration party when we returned to the village."

Miles laughed, but suddenly his laugh stuck in his throat. He felt an eerie prickle at the back of his neck. They were not alone. He turned around slowly and was frozen with fear. "Oh, no. I think that party will have to wait."

Chapter 7:
ATTACK OF THE CULTISTS

A sher and Owen saw the look on Miles's face before they saw the four quiet, blue-robed figures standing menacingly before them—two with bows and arrows and two bowing and waving their arms around. "What in the world?" Asher said in disbelief. "Are these guys for real?"

"I think they're cultists," Miles said quietly, afraid to disturb them. They stood in front of the three warriors. One was holding a mysterious tablet.

Owen cocked his head sideways to get a better look at the tablet. "Whatcha got there? I can't seem to read what it is."

"Don't touch them. You'll start a fight," Miles warned.

"What?" Owen asked mischievously reaching out his finger to touch one of the blue robes. "You mean I can't do this?"

The quiet figures immediately sprang to life. One of the archers began shooting arrows at the group. Fortunately, Miles was still wearing his protective armor and had his shield ready. The arrow bounced off his shield to a ledge, which knocked a rock free. The rock rolled down the ledge, took a high bounce and landed on the blue cultist archer, instantly defeating him. Miles looked around in surprise to make sure he hadn't imagined it. "Did that really just happen?"

Asher and Owen nodded enthusiastically. "Best deflection ever!" Owen said.

"Watch out, there's another one!" Asher called. He grabbed for his broadsword but it got caught in his pack. The archer aimed his weapon directly at Asher, ready to fire, as Asher struggled with his weapon. Just then, Miles crept up behind the archer and took him out with his broadsword. The archer fell, unleashing his arrow into the sky.

As Owen helped Asher free his sword, Miles quickly dispatched the other two cultists, who silently disappeared. He then walked over to Asher and un-snagged his blade from his pack with one easy movement. "You guys didn't plan that whole thing to get my confidence back, did you?" Miles asked suspiciously. "Because it was almost too convenient . . ."

Asher and Owen denied having anything to do with it. "We wouldn't put ourselves in danger just to make you feel better, Miles," Asher explained. "We're nice but we're not dumb."

"I guess you're right," Miles said.

"Of course he's right," Owen replied. "We were in trouble and you helped us. It couldn't be easier to understand. Don't start making up ways to make yourself feel better about hanging up your sword. You're a great warrior, whether you want to be or not. That's why I followed you when I met you."

"I thought you followed me because you wanted a new guide," Miles said.

"First I watched you. I saw how you handled your weapons. How you made smart decisions when you had time, but how you used your quick reflexes when you needed to. I followed you because you're good," Owen explained.

Miles turned so they couldn't see his face redden with embarrassment. "Well, thanks, guys. Thanks for coming back for me and thanks for . . ." But Miles didn't get to finish his speech. Another blue-robed figure entered the altar room. But this one was not bowing or holding arrows. Its face was ghostly, with a long nose, black piercing eyes, and a strong presence that made all three warriors feel like they were facing a great and ancient power. "It's The Lunatic Cultist," Miles whispered softly. "Whatever you do, don't attack."

"I won't even touch its sleeve," Owen replied in a whisper.

"The Ancient Cultist, fanatical leader of the dungeon coven, will counter any attack with a rain of fire, ice, or electric currents, according to the legend. The Dao of Pow has nothing on this guy—he can duplicate himself to create decoys of Ancient Cultists and if you strike the wrong one . . . well, you'll end up in your own bed so fast it'll make your head spin," Miles continued quietly, recalling one of his least favorite ghost stories from childhood.

"What will it do if we don't do anything to it?" Asher asked. "Can it hurt us?"

"No. It'll only fight back if we attack. If we don't, it will despawn and we'll have to fight those blue-robed archers and devotees again tomorrow." Miles led them out of the room toward the dungeon and sure enough the mob despawned with a pop.

"Now that we know what we're up against, it'll be easy, right?" Owen said hopefully as they walked.

"Yep. And when you guys are ready, you can fight the boss, start the Lunar Events and defeat the Celestial Towers, but that is a hard boss battle I have no intention of fighting now or ever," Miles said.

"You'll eat those words, buddy. You always come back to the sword," Asher said with a laugh as they rose up to the surface. The sky was bright and clear. The calm of an early morning just after dawn was a relief after the nightmares they had faced in the underground jungle. Miles wasn't sure where they were and spun around in circles, unsure which way was home.

Owen reached into his inventory and pulled out a compass. "Home is this way," he pointed to the left uncertainly.

"Are you sure you're reading it right?" Asher asked grabbing at it to check.

Owen snatched it back, annoyed. "You don't trust me to read a compass?"

As they argued Miles looked up ahead and saw a castle. It looked familiar. Miles couldn't place it but he had an uneasy feeling. "Owen, I have to agree with Asher. I don't think we went the right way," he said.

Owen looked at his compass and shook it. Asher grabbed it and turned it around. "You were looking at it upside down, Owen," he said shaking his head. Then he looked up at the castle. "I think I've been here before, a long time ago."

"Me too," Owen said nervously, walking up to the castle door. "I want to go in, but I'm scared.

"Then we should definitely go in!" Asher said.

As Asher approached the door, a message appeared: *"Screams are echoing from the dungeon."*

"That sounds scary . . ." Owen said.

"Are you guys up for another adventure? I am!"" Asher asked as he turned the handle and the door creaked open.

"I guess we don't have a choice, now," Miles said sullenly.

Chapter 8:

WHAT HAPPENS IN THE DUNGEON, STAYS IN THE DUNGEON

Asher walked in and stopped cold in his tracks. "Skeletron."

Owen whipped around nervously clutching his blade. "What? Where? Not again!"

Suddenly Miles remembered. "Right—this was the dungeon where I defeated Skeletron."

"Me too," Owen and Asher replied at the same time.

"This was one of the first tasks on the way to enter hardmode," Asher recalled. "It feels like a lifetime ago."

Miles suddenly felt small and embarrassed. He had been going through his adventures thinking he was the only one who was chosen to be a warrior, and the only one who had defeated Skeletron and the Wall of Flesh to get to this point. Asher and Owen had faced the same trials to get here. They were treating him as the expert, but really they all had earned the right to be called warriors after all they had been through. While all he really wanted was to go home and start fishing, he could read Asher and Owen's excitement so plainly on their faces. Miles decided to hang back and let the other two take the lead as they entered the dungeon. As he walked in behind them, he saw that they were standing at the mouth of a labyrinth—a large maze that Miles knew would lead underground. "Watch out for traps," Miles cautioned them before he remembered he wasn't going to direct them.

Owen pulled out his wrench and the wires lit up as they had before. "Thanks, Miles!" he called cheerfully, ducking and weaving around the traps and collecting the wires.

Asher gave Miles an appreciative nod. "You saved us once again." Miles grimaced. He'd have to remember to hold his tongue. If he kept warning them about dangers before they encountered them, they'd never learn on their own.

Their footsteps echoed through the corridors. Owen activated a lantern switch on the cave wall that lit up the area around them. Suddenly, Asher grew alert. "Listen, do you hear that?" Miles heard a squish that sounded like a slime. He nodded. Asher whipped around and was faced with an indigo slime, rare and unusual in a dungeon but very helpful, Miles recalled. Asher hadn't pulled out his weapon in time and was hit by the slime, taking damage. He fell to the ground clutching his arm. "Didn't see that coming," he grimaced.

The slime bounced up and was about to hit Owen when Miles drew his sword and sliced it mid-air. It fell to the ground and disappeared, leaving a golden key behind.

Owen picked it up and handed it to Miles. "Thanks, buddy. Here. You earned this."

"Add another save to your belt," Asher said quietly as he waited for his healing potion to kick in. He sounded proud of Miles, not resentful as Miles would have expected.

"It was nothing," Miles mumbled, helping Asher to his feet. "You would've done the same for me." They walked on through the labyrinth, deactivating traps and turning on light switches as they went. It was easy going once you knew the dangers to avoid, Miles thought. Experience was a great teacher.

Owen stopped at a golden chest. "I think this chest matches your key, Miles." Miles handed the key to Owen to open the chest but Owen shook his head. "You try it. You've earned it."

Miles shrugged and popped in the key, fighting the urge to flinch in case it was a mimic. He had to stop being so cautious and embrace the challenges of the adventure! The chest opened to reveal a large stash of coins that glowed in the lamplight.

"You really hit the jackpot, Miles," Asher said with a low whistle.

"We hit the jackpot, you mean," Miles said, dividing the treasure into three equal bags and handing two to his companions. "Three amigos, right?"

Owen and Asher accepted the bounty gratefully. Their thanks were interrupted by a banging sound. Miles grabbed his repeater from his inventory. Asher noticed and pulled out the Nettle Burst. Owen grabbed his Megashark. They nodded silently at each other, knowing enemies were just around the corner. Sure enough, a Paladin emerged from the shadows, swinging its hammer. Asher dodged out of the way while Owen shot it with the Megashark, crippling its attack.

As they inched forward carefully, Owen spotted another chest covered with green vines. "I think this is the jungle chest," he said. It matched the key he had collected when they defeated Plantera.

"Try it and see," Miles said encouragingly. Owen fit the key into the lock and turned it. The chest opened to reveal a Piranha Gun. "Nice!" Owen shouted, examining the weapon to see what it could do.

Miles heard a noise approaching from his right. He turned to see an evil-looking skeleton-faced creature wearing a robe. "Caster!" he called out, recognizing it from a poster of dangerous creatures the demolitionist kept on his wall. Miles shot his repeater at The Caster, but the knockback damage was too low. The Caster fired three shots back, hitting Miles on the leg. Miles was instantly blinded. The world turned black and he could hear a loud pop.

"I got it!" Asher called out. Miles heard a burst of fire and heard The Caster drop. His vision cleared in time to see Asher picking up its drops: a golden key, a bone, and a sack full of coins. He grinned wildly. "Saved you this time! Starting to even the score." Miles didn't have time to thank him. Another enemy appeared—a Diabolist—with a grey robe and evil red eyes. It shot a fire bolt that whizzed past Miles's ear, then disappeared, reappearing in another corner of the room.

Owen raised his Pirhana Gun and aimed it at the Diabolist, shooting before it could release another fireball. The piranha ammunition targeted the Diabolist, latched on, and didn't let go until its job was done. Owen let out a happy shout. "I LOVE THIS WEAPON!" Even in the heat of the battle, Asher and Miles laughed before turning to face the giant cursed skulls that had passed through the walls and were homing in for an attack. Asher raised his Nettle Burst and took out three while Miles finished the last two off with his repeater.

Breathlessly they recharged their weapons and retreated to a corner of the dungeon room. Miles brought out a stack of healing potion and doled it out to his companions, drinking some himself. His supplies were getting low, but he couldn't place the heart statue since they needed to travel. A slime bounced in and Miles shot it halfheartedly, destroying it with a blast of fire.

"Nice shot," Owen said, sounding tired, reaching out a bruised hand to pick up the gold key it had dropped. "Is there any place to hide from these enemies while we recover?"

"I'm afraid not," Miles said. "Lots of things down here seem to travel through walls and teleport after they shoot."

Asher shook his head. "I thought we were prepared for anything, but I don't think I can take much more of this."

Miles was inclined to agree, but they still had to plot their escape. Up and out seemed the only way to go, but how would they get through more of these ghostly enemies? "I think we should retreat." Both of his friends nodded and looked at him expectantly. It was clear they wanted him to make the plan, but Miles was tired, hungry, and hurt, and his mind was blank. They were trapped and no matter how he looked at it, they weren't getting out of there without a fight.

Chapter 9:
SPIRITS IN THE NIGHT

Miles checked his inventory and noticed one of his friends from the village had thrown in some snacks when he wasn't looking. Happy he had such thoughtful friends, he tossed each of his companions an apple and they munched quietly as they figured out what to do. Miles kept his repeater out as he ate, absently blasting anything that flew into the room so they could concentrate on a plan.

What he hadn't counted on was the dungeon spirits. As Miles's defeated enemy count mounted, ghostlike creatures started appearing, floating dangerously close to their heads. As his repeater recharged, he shot his Crystal Storm at a nearby enemy, hoping the confused debuff would send him in the opposite direction and buy him time. The enemy kept at him, though, and hit him with full force. He felt cold and weak as the spirit passed through him. Asher blasted the enemy, saving Miles from another attack. With a grateful nod to Asher, Miles drank his last remaining potion and raised his repeater to avoid any more hits. He collected the coins and ectoplasm dropped by the enemy and handed them to Asher. "What was that thing?"

"If you don't know, we certainly don't," Owen replied, taking out another one as it melted through the wall into the room.

"It's a ghost of some kind, that's clear. A dungeon ghost, maybe?" Asher offered, taking out his bow and arrow and loosing a stream of arrows at an approaching skeleton.

"Right! A dungeon spirit. They only come out when we kill difficult enemies," Miles remembered.

"Boy, all that reading really gave you an education about all these mobs," Asher observed. "That knowledge would have been wasted if you stayed in town farming and fishing."

Miles had to agree he was right, but he still just wanted to go home and stand down from high alert. He had to get them out of the dungeon and above ground before they lost everything. "Let's just get out of here, okay? We'll finish this conversation later."

Owen checked his compass and pointed to the far wall. "I think we should go this way." Miles and Asher looked at him. "No, really, it's right side up now. It's this way."

Miles shrugged. "I trust you. It's better than staying in this room and being targets for whatever comes our way." They walked out of the room and down a narrow hallway. Miles noticed Asher was limping slightly, but when he asked him about it, Asher shrugged it off and put his finger to his lips, signaling that they should be quiet. He motioned to take the left path in a fork they came to. Miles and Owen nodded and followed him. They entered a dead end filled with skeletons shooting arrows and fireballs at them. "Retreat!" Miles called, ushering them out behind him as he shot as many as he could with his repeater on his way out.

Owen threw up a brick wall, sealing in the remaining enemies. They took the other path and made their way up to the surface. Flying dungeon spirits came at them from all sides and they each unleashed their weapons to quickly take care of the mob before collecting the coins and drops.

"We need to start disabling mobs instead of destroying them if we want the dungeon spirits to stop coming at us," Miles observed. "They only appear after we get rid of a high-level mob."

"Good point," Asher said, rubbing honey on his leg.

"You're hurt," Owen said to Asher.

"We all have injuries," Asher said, trying to sound casual.

"We have to get out of here now," Miles said. He looked around. "We've been in this room before," he noticed. "The way out is through this corridor." He pointed to the exit.

A horde of skeletons appeared behind them. Owen threw up another wall, blocking the skeletons' path. "Let's get out of here!" he shouted, leading the way to the exit.

The three warriors escaped from the dungeon, closing the door behind them and sprinting toward home. As they stopped and caught their breath, Miles pointed at the moon shining above them. "I don't think the danger is behind us."

As if on cue, a horde of zombies came into view. "Weapons ready!" Asher called, pulling out his Megashark and firing at the crowd. Miles pulled out his repeater and hit two zombies and Owen hit three with his bow and arrow. Miles didn't know if he could take much more combat. He was so tired, his bones ached, and he missed the comfort of his bed.

As a new wave of zombies started to approach the trio, the sky lightened. In a few moments, any remaining zombies would sizzle in the sunlight and they would be free to go home. It was their first stroke of luck since leaving home. Miles, Owen, and Asher breathed a sigh of relief as the sun rose on the forest and the zombies disappeared.

Chapter 10:
HOME AGAIN

Bathed in the early morning sunlight, the three warriors made their way back to the village in silence. Each one was thinking about what they were looking forward to when they returned home. Owen was thinking of the party. Asher was looking forward to replenishing his supplies and getting a good rest before heading back out to face The Lunatic Cultist. Miles wanted to get back to his farm, go fishing, and catch up on some reading so he could prepare Asher and Owen for their next adventures.

After a while, the terrain became more familiar. They didn't need the help of a map or compass to know they were on the right path toward home. Miles knew he had left some things unsaid back in the dungeon and he realized this was the right time to bring it up. He wasn't much for speeches or admitting he was wrong, but he owed that much to Asher and Owen. He cleared his throat, unsure how to begin. "Um . . . You were right back there."

Asher raised his eyebrows in surprise. "What's that? I was what?"

Miles grinned. "Right. You were right. Even though we got hurt pretty badly and used up our Mana and got attacked by spirits and angry mobs, I'm glad I stuck it out."

Asher and Owen high fived. "Knew it!" Owen said. "You love this stuff!"

"I do. In small amounts," Miles admitted. "This was a great vacation, but I'm ready to go back . . ." He didn't get to finish his sentence. They were all distracted by a flying object that buzzed past them. "What's that?" The other two shrugged in response. They ran over to get a better look.

"If I didn't know better, I'd swear it was a spaceship," Owen said scratching his head. "I must be really tired!" They all laughed and continued on their way home, their spirits lifted at the sight of the familiar landscape.

"I'm so hungry, I could eat a feast right now," Owen said, licking his lips at the thought of the feast that awaited successful warriors. Bunny the party girl was definitely going to cook up something amazing for them on their return. In fact, Owen thought he could smell smoke, and smoke usually meant one thing: cooking! "Any chance they knew we were coming and started cooking up something for us ahead of time?" he asked, pointing at the column of smoke that he now saw clearly rising above the treeline.

Miles and Asher shrugged and quickened their steps, concerned that the smoke wasn't from a cooking grill. Their village had burned once before, thanks to Asher's mischief, and Miles wasn't keen on rebuilding it a third time, with or without the help of his companions.

A message appeared in front of them: "*Martians are invading!*"

"It WAS a spaceship!" Owen said in a voice filled with panic. "What do we do?"

"We run and help!" Miles replied, drawing his weapon and running at top speed through the trees toward the village.

As the trio came into the clearing, they saw a fleet of alien ships hovering above the village square. Their friends were gathered at the top of the hill, back to back, weapons drawn and ready for the attack.

"We're here to help!" Asher shouted as they approached. As soon as Miles entered the village, the attack began.

A saucer bobbed above Miles's head and Autumn the mechanic threw her wrench at it to knock it away. "It's about time. These saucers have been hovering for a while and threatening to attack as soon as you arrived. We're just glad you're here so we can get rid of them."

A storm of missiles rained down as the saucer bobbed and weaved around their heads. Aliens were dropping down to attack. The group was outnumbered and outclassed with weapons. The villagers were trying to stand their ground but their weapons were clearly no match for the alien attack.

"Quick, everybody, get into a shelter," Miles shouted, running for his house. "We'll be safe from the saucer attack from here and we can get into formation." The villagers and warriors followed Miles's lead. He was glad he had expanded his house by several floors since he was spending more time at home.

Asher looked around the house. It was clear he wasn't impressed. "That's it? That's your plan, to hide out in your cozy little shack until the Martian invasion is over?"

Miles laughed. "It's funny you'd think that about me after everything we've been through." He opened the basement door. "Follow me and have your ranged weapon ready." Miles led Asher to his proudest achievement—a bunker underneath the house with everything he needed to launch a below-ground attack.

Asher entered the bunker and smiled. "You built it into a cliff, you sly devil!"

Owen followed behind. "If I had a house like this, I might just stay close to home too."

Danny the angler wandered in. "If I had a house like this, I'd stay too."

Miles smacked his forehead. "Danny! I haven't forgotten about you, I promise. I'm sorry it's taking me so long to build you a—"

Danny jumped up and down with excitement. "Are you kidding me? I love it here! I'm not going anywhere. There are aliens invading! How cool is that?"

Miles laughed. "I'm glad you like it here. Now get somewhere safe, out of the way, and I'll come get you when the danger's over."

"Sure thing!" Danny said, then wandered back upstairs. "I'm going to make you an aquarium while I wait."

Miles showed Asher and Owen to the edge of the cliff where he had built protective see-through barriers. "From down here, I can see anything coming at me from ground or sky."

As Danny went back upstairs, the other villagers swarmed in. Some suited up with armor and weapons, ready to head out into the battlefield while Jack the demolitionist, Hope the steampunker, and Cedric the wizard stayed on the front lines with the warriors. It was clear from the way they took their places in formation that this wasn't the first invasion they had faced.

"Everyone ready?" Miles called out.

All the villagers responded as if with one voice. "Ready, Miles!"

"Let's do this!" Miles shouted. The armored villagers ran outside in formation, fanning out across the landscape in pairs. One partner provided shelter and protection with bricks or blocks while the other began to shoot at the enemies swarming in.

Miles turned to Owen and Asher. "Get out your ranged weapons. Use anything that can shoot through glass or blocks. If you don't have one, head to the far corner and shoot from behind a barrier. Keep backup weapons on hand, got it?"

Asher and Owen snapped to attention. Miles was in charge and everyone was on board with his plan.

Asher turned to Owen and whispered: "There might just be a chance we can win this with Miles in charge."

Chapter 11:
SPACE INVADERS

Miles aimed his Nettle Burst through the wall of glass, targeting the main alien ship. Owen unleashed the piranha from his gun at the nearest alien—a three-legged Martian walker that shot a constant stream of lasers. The piranha latched on to the walker, taking out each of its legs, then destroying the body before heading back to Owen's gun for another launch. "Have I mentioned lately that I LOVE this weapon?" Owen shouted gleefully.

Asher took cover behind a barrier at the far end of the bunker and released a barrage of ammunition from his Megashark, taking out a handful of green, gray, and red aliens. With each drop, more loot appeared on the ground. Miles knew without even looking that Asher was staring at the loot, thinking about how he could safely collect it before anyone else. "Leave the loot, Asher. You'll get yourself killed if you head out there now."

Asher laughed. "Yeah, I know. But just look at it!"

"Look out!" Miles shouted as a laser from the spaceship shot in the open space above Asher's head.

Asher's hair smoked from a brush with the laser. His eyes were wide open in surprise. "That was way too close for comfort. I'm suiting up and heading outside where it's safer!" He headed to the armory and grabbed some palladium armor, a shield, and two repeaters. "This should hold me."

"Wait, you need a buddy," Miles said. "I'll come with you." He handed his Nettle Burst to Owen. "Owen, you stay here. You're the most accurate shooter. Focus on the spaceship, then keep an eye on our team and target any alien that looks like it's causing trouble for our friends."

"Got it, boss," Owen said, putting down his Piranha Gun and shouldering the Nettle Burst.

"Oh, one more thing," Miles said. "The Tesla Turrets."

"The what?" Owen asked distractedly. He was already firing at the approaching hordes of aliens and had taken out three without blinking an eye.

"The Tesla Turrets," Miles repeated. "Super important. The Martian engineer will leave behind a machine that shoots off an electricity debuff. They drop them everywhere, and if you don't take them out right away, we're all doomed."

"Doomed?" Asher snorted. "Are you sure you're not exaggerating?"

"If you're hit with it, you take damage every time you move. Every step," Miles replied angrily. "In less than a dozen steps, it'll take you out and you'll end up back in your cozy little bed, far from your precious loot, so no, I'm not exaggerating."

"Man, you can get touchy in the heat of battle," Asher said, heading up to the battleground. "Come on, let's take some of that anger out on those little green men!"

Miles suited up in his best armor, grabbed two repeaters and a shield, and followed Asher to the surface. A green ray gunner ran past them as they exited the shelter. He fired two laser blasts, just missing them, then retreated to another corner of the field. The alien ship was firing lasers rapid-fire, setting small fires across the land. It was amazing how a small village could turn into a flaming battleground so quickly.

"I hate it when my village gets attacked," Miles said as he took out a nearby gray alien. "Rebuilding is such a pain, and the villagers have more requests each time."

"They should really start helping you build," Asher suggested. "Hey, why does that one have a helmet?" he asked, pointing at a nearby alien.

"Beats me," Miles said, just before he got hit with its ray. He suddenly felt confused. He tried to turn to face Asher to see if he had gotten hit too, but he turned the wrong way. He took a step toward the house, but ended up walking away. "ho hU," he said instead of Uh oh. He had been hit by a confused debuff. "desufnoC," he tried to tell Asher, but it all came out backward.

Miles knew it would only last a few moments, but moments were precious in the middle of the battle. He willed himself to do the opposite of what he wanted to do, lowering his gun instead of raising it and pointing it away from the helmeted brain scrambler alien. He unfired the gun and heard a pop signaling it was a perfect shot. Miles frowned, leaving a smile on his face. This backwards confused stuff was hard to master! Fortunately, his head cleared quickly. Just in time to see an alien headed toward them at top speed riding a green dinosaur-like beast.

"Hey, that's a Scutlix," Asher said, pointing at the beast. "I knew a guy who kept one for a pet. Rode it everywhere." He pointed his Megashark at the alien rider. "Best way to travel, he said." He fired at the alien and missed. "Drat. Missed. I want to get one of those. Two or three, even, so we can all ride together." He fired two more times. The first shot missed completely. The second hit the Scutlix, freeing the rider to run straight at them, firing his lasers. "Drat!" Asher said. "Missed again."

Miles took the approaching alien out quickly with his repeater. "Let's not worry about the Scutlix, okay? We have bigger fish—or aliens—to fry!"

A Martian engineer ran by them, dropping a machine in front of them that appeared to be sparking with electricity. "Tesla Turret!" Asher cried. "Owen, help!" Owen replied from inside with a blast that obliterated the Turret. "Thanks!" Asher called out and ran to help Katie and Isabella fend off a horde of aliens closing in on them.

"Wait up!" Miles called, running after him. A Martian walker strode over him and filled up its charge. Miles dove and rolled out of the way, narrowly escaping its laser. Miles wheeled around and shot it with his laser. It was a direct hit, but the walker kept approaching. "How does this thing have no knockback?" he yelled in frustration. Fortunately, Owen had his back and obliterated the walker with a direct hit. Miles waved an arm in thanks, then ran to join Asher in helping the nurse and the dryad fend off their attackers.

After an intense exchange of fire with the aliens, the crowd finally seemed to thin out. Isaac the Goblin tinkerer, Autumn the mechanic, and the rest of the villagers came over to focus their attack on the ship. One electrified alien strode into the group and zapped Bunny the party girl, shocking her with an electricity debuff. She landed on the ground, shaking. Hope ran over and took care of her. Asher blasted the zapper who hit Bunny. "You can't hit our friend! Take that!"

The rest of the villagers closed in and threw all the ammunition they had at the Martian saucer and the remaining aliens. With a huge explosion, the saucer was zapped out of existence. The villagers let out a whoop of excitement as Danny, Owen, and the rest of the group ran from the house to join the celebration.

"We did it!" Autumn shouted. "We beat the Martian Invasion!"

Hope and Isaac gently lifted Bunny from the ground. She was weak but her cheeks were regaining their color and she looked like she was already feeling better. "I'm going to throw one heck of a party to celebrate this victory!" she said.

"I'll help!" Danny called out. "I love parties!"

While the villagers prepared for the party, Asher, Owen, and Miles cleaned up the battlefield. "There are enough Martian blocks here to make a whole house!" Asher said.

"That's great! I bet Danny would love a house built with Martian plates. They pulse in the dark, so it would even make a great night light!" Miles said, happily collecting the plates and putting them aside.

"There's a ton of useless costume junk here in case anyone wants to dress up like a Martian,"

Owen observed, picking up the discarded alien clothing and throwing it in another pile.

Miles picked up a gun and inspected it. "I think this is the brain scrambler that the alien used on me to make me confused." He handed it to Asher. "I already have a Crystal Storm which does the same thing, so you take this one."

"Thanks," Asher said. "Owen and I can share it. It'll help us when we go back and battle those Lunatic Cultists." Asher picked up a trophy and handed it to Miles. "You can keep this since you're the one with a fancy house. We nomads don't need decoration."

"Don't give that to me!" Miles pushed it away. "It's not for decoration. It's to summon another Martian attack! Let's destroy it!"

"Let's bury it instead," Owen suggested. "You never know when you need to hitch a ride on a flying saucer!"

As the trio collected the rest of the loot, including a Cosmic Car Key, some blasters and lasers, an Anti-Gravity Hook, a cannon, and a lot of healing potion, the rest of the crew were preparing a feast. Wonderful smells were coming from the house and they realized they hadn't eaten a proper meal in a long time. They went indoors to discover disco lights, music, and decorations. Bunny met them at the door with party hats and a glass of something fizzy and sweet.

"Now this is my kind of party!" Asher exclaimed, joining a conga line behind Roland the clothier. But before anyone could dig into the feast, Miles spotted something out of the corner of his eye. He looked out the window but didn't see anything.

Owen saw it too. He met Miles at the window. "That was another scout ship, wasn't it?"

Miles nodded. "It's a probe, alright. Looks like it's too soon for a celebration. Our party will have to wait. Again."

Chapter 12:
THE NEXT WAVE

Miles and Owen pulled Asher from the dance floor where he was trying to master the art of the electric slide dance. "Hey, I almost have it down. What gives?" Asher asked angrily.

"Come with us. We need you to see something," Miles said into Asher's ear. He didn't want to disrupt the villagers' hard-earned fun with more bad news. Miles took Asher to the window where Owen was waiting.

"The scout hasn't detected us yet," Owen said.

"That's good news," Miles replied. "That gives us time to plan our next defense."

"I'd rather plan an attack than a defense," Owen said thoughtfully. "Now that we know what to expect, we can take proper advantage of the attack and get maximum drop with minimum damage."

"Excellent point, Owen!" Miles said proudly. He was glad Owen had learned how important advance planning can be in a battle.

Asher had been following the conversation, looking back and forth between his two friends as they spoke as if watching a tennis match. "What exactly are you talking about?" he asked, finally.

Owen pointed at the probe bobbing off in the distance. "It's still green, which means it hasn't spotted us yet."

Asher's eyes lit up with excitement. "You mean we get another shot at these guys? Anyone know where we can find some water candles?"

"You want to increase their spawn rate?" Miles asked. "We could barely keep up with them in the last wave."

"But you guys said we could plan our defense. Let's try it. I want more loot!" Asher replied, rubbing his hands together greedily.

Miles looked to Owen for support. "You agree this is crazy, right?"

Owen shook his head. "Actually, no. This is a great opportunity for us to see what we can really do. We have the support of all of the villagers, we're here on your home turf, and we actually have advance notice this time that an attack is on the way."

Miles considered what they had said. He had to admit their points were strong. If the Martians were coming anyway, they might as well get the most out of the attack. He just had one thing left to do. Miles looked around for a platform to address his friends, but not finding one, he climbed up on a nearby table and held his hands up to get everyone's attention. "Excuse me! I'd like to say something!"

"Here's where he's going to thank us for our loyalty and congratulate us on a job well done," Isaac whispered to Autumn, eagerly expecting the praise.

"I want to thank you all for your bravery and support in this difficult Martian battle. We couldn't have done this without every one of you," Miles said. A cheer went up around the room. Isaac nudged Autumn who seemed impressed that he called it so perfectly. "Unfortunately, this was just the first wave." The group broke out in a collective groan. "A probe was spotted nearby, and once it finds me, Owen, and Asher here in the village, the aliens will return."

Hope gasped. "I'm going to need a lot more honey and supplies," she said to no one in particular.

Jack the demolitionist checked his pockets to make sure they were full of weapons. "We can handle it," he said.

Katie checked her armor for holes or damage. "We're ready for it when you are," she shouted supportively.

"I was going to ask if you guys were up for the challenge, but it seems we already have our answer," Miles said to the crowd. They cheered in response. Isabella raised her hands at one edge of the group and shouted: "Here's to the next wave! Let's start a wave!" In response, the villagers each raised their hands one at a time and cheered, showing a wave of support. It went around the group twice before Miles held up his own hands to stop them. "I'm glad you're all in! But here's the thing, we want to plan ahead. The attack won't start if we're not in the village, so we actually have time to prepare for this."

Hope the steampunker raised her clockwork assault rifle in support. "I'm with you, Miles!" she shouted. Autumn raised her wrench and Bunny fired her confetti gun, showering the crowd with colorful confetti. "Let's move this party out of town. I'm not going to put up with any party crashers! Anyone who's with us, grab some party supplies and follow me!" Bunny shouted. She led the group outside of the party room in a conga line carrying a bowl of fruit on her head.

Miles fell in line behind her carrying the disco ball. "Where are we going?"

"Outside the village to prepare while we party, silly," she replied with a toss of her ponytail. "I can rally troops like the best of them. I have everyone behind you now."

Miles turned to see that, in fact, all of the villagers and Owen and Asher were actually following them out of the village and into the nearby forest. Each person was carrying something from the party as they danced. "Nice work, Bunny!" Miles said appreciatively. They could party and plan at the same time.

Once they were in the clearing, Owen searched the skies for the probe. He spotted it hovering over Cedric the wizard's green hut at the edge of the village. The light was still green, but the probe didn't show any signs of giving up the search. He reported back to Miles.

"Great," Miles said. "The last thing we need is to prepare for an invasion only to have the probe get impatient and leave before we get to do any fighting!" He decided they had some time to spare so he could give everyone time to enjoy themselves before he started shouting out orders.

The group was chatting excitedly and enjoying the new party venue. Sarah the stylist helped Bunny string the lights around the clearing while Isabella the dryad threw a wall of protective vines around them for good measure and to add some pretty decoration to the party. Miles didn't join in the fun. He decided instead to run through the last battle in his mind, thinking of ways to stop the aliens and counter the attacks.

From what he remembered, there were several types of aliens attacking all at once. The saucer shot out a steady stream of lasers, but the lasers couldn't get through walls. The walker was like a walking version of the saucer, only smaller. The turret would electrify anyone in the area, so all turrets needed to be taken out as soon as the engineer placed them. He'd probably need a dedicated turret gunner. The drone seemed like an annoying bug that would explode like a bomb given the opportunity, but he wasn't sure yet how it would behave in a fight. The rest of the enemies were Martians, and they had different jobs and levels of protection. Their danger seemed to be in their numbers, not necessarily their strength.

Miles calculated they'd need a roof overhead, a gunner for the turret, traps for the Martians and lots of weapons on hand to keep them safe.

Confident he had a good read of the situation, he scanned the party space for his companions. Asher was being lifted on a chair in the center of the dance floor by Isaac and Autumn as the rest of the group crowded around and cheered. Who knew Asher would be such a major party animal?! Cedric the wizard was happily shooting off colorful fireworks inside the vine canopy. Miles found Owen at the edge of the clearing, searching the skies for the probe. "How's it looking?" Miles asked, joining him at the lookout point.

"Still hovering. Still green," Owen reported. "This thing's patient, but it has picked up speed and it seems to be getting a little bolder, going lower in the sky to make sure we're not hiding somewhere."

Miles nodded. "Okay. Sounds like we don't have much time before it spots us out here, especially with Cedric's fireworks going off inside the canopy." As soon as he spoke, a burst of blue and purple sparks erupted from Cedric's arsenal. It was met by ooh's and aah's from the crowd. "Here's what I've figured so far." Miles recapped his thoughts to Owen about the battle and they began outlining a plan.

Soon, Asher spotted them in the corner and came over. He was wearing a party hat and his clothes were covered in confetti. "What's up, party poopers?" he asked, draping an arm around each of his friends' shoulders. "Having fun being boring?"

Miles smiled and gently shrugged off Asher's arm. "Glad you're having a good time, but unfortunately, the party's about to be over."

Asher removed his party hat and shook off the confetti. He was suddenly all business. "Okay. What have you got so far?"

Miles and Owen outlined the plan they were beginning to put together. It was a solid plan of defense, Asher had to agree, but it didn't have any of the attack skills that Owen had suggested, and there was no opportunity to farm aliens and rack up their drops. "You've gotten good at defending yourself, Miles. You're becoming a great villager. But you have to remember how to think like a warrior again," Asher reminded him gently. "Look, old pal, we can avoid the battle entirely if you want. We can wait long enough and the probe will go off on its merry way and leave us alone for good if that's what you want." Asher looked Miles in the eye. "Is that what you want? Because you need to make a choice, and you need to make it right now."

Chapter 13:
MARTIAN MADNESS

Miles didn't need to think it over. He knew Asher was right. He had to get his head back in the game. He wasn't about to give up a fight before it even began. "Did either of you bring a workbench?" he asked. "I have a candle and some water. All we need is your crystal ball and we have ourselves a water candle."

"Yes!" Asher replied, hugging Miles. "Miles the warrior is back!"

Owen reached into his inventory and pulled out a workbench. "Now we have what we need. Let's craft that mob-farming alien magnet of a water candle!"

The three friends crafted other items and pulled their friends in one at a time to purchase supplies for the fight. They didn't stop the party until the last possible moment. When everyone was fed and rested and the party space had been cleaned up, they were ready for the fight. The mood had grown quiet and expectant. A big change from the festive atmosphere of the party just minutes earlier. "Everyone know what they have to do?" Miles asked. The group murmured in agreement. They each checked their supplies, fixed their armor and lined up to head back to the village. "Remember, as soon as the probe sees us, the attack will begin."

Miles led the march into battle, holding his Crystal Storm rod more for visual effect than military effectiveness. A confusion debuff wouldn't cause much damage—it would just buy them time—but it looked good to lead the charge with such an imposing magical weapon.

As soon as they entered the village clearing, the probe spotted them. It turned red. "This is your last chance to get out of this," Asher whispered to Miles. "Let it escape and it's all over."

"Not a chance," Miles replied, his jaw set tight in resolve. He holstered the Crystal Storm and pulled out the Nettle Burst, obliterating the Martian probe with one shot.

A status message appeared once again: "Martians are invading!"

The villagers quickly sprang into action. Autumn the mechanic and Isaac the tinkerer dug a trench and filled it with lava. They built an altar for the water candle just beyond the pit. Meanwhile, Carlo the painter, Sarah the stylist, Roland the tailor and Bunny the party girl built a tall and very stylish platform with a wide roof. Carlo and Roland almost got into a fistfight over whether the stairs should be cobalt blue or sky blue, but fortunately Sarah stepped in and got them to compromise with alternating stripes of each color.

Katie set up an infirmary at the clearing and asked Danny to help her harvest as much honey as he could to have on hand for healing during the battle.

As the teams worked to build their battle arena, John the merchant and Jack the demolitionist joined Asher and Owen on the roof of Jack's house to defend against the first wave of attacks. Miles walked among the groups, checking on supplies and helping out where he could. He had his repeater ready for the first sign of a walking enemy as they prepared, knowing that the attack could begin at any time.

Just as the team was completing the roof of the structure and everyone was getting into position, the Martian saucer appeared, raining down lasers on the village. Cedric panicked and summoned a vase of flowers instead of his flower of fire. Fortunately, Isabella was nearby and threw up a protective wall around him as he sorted himself out. "Thank you, Carmella," the wizard said gratefully to the dryad. She smiled at the unusual name he gave her. As she fixed her gaze on the sky, she wondered absently if Cedric mixed up everyone's names on purpose. But then she looked down at the poor wizard trying to herd a family of bunnies back into his hat and realized the poor man wasn't nearly that calculating.

Fortunately, Isaac and Autumn were more pre-pared than the wizard. At the first sign of alien invaders on the ground, Isaac threw a spiky ball at the oncoming trio. The ball bounced three times, taking out all of the aliens in one shot. Meanwhile, at his side, Autumn tossed her wrench at an oncom-ing walker, taking out one of its three legs. The walker tottered forward as the wrench returned to Autumn's hand and she threw it again, taking out the alien's second leg. Autumn realized too late she had miscalculated her attack. The alien fell forward like a tree being chopped down, and it was falling toward Autumn. Isaac rushed over at the last min-ute and pushed Autumn out of the way of the fall-ing walker. He threw a spiky ball at the alien's head, obliterating it. Autumn sat stunned, realizing Isaac had saved her from certain death. "Thank you," she said breathlessly. "You saved my life."

The goblin's green face turned bright pink with embarrassment. "Think nothing of it. These aliens are a lot harder to defeat than evil goblins. Are you hurt?" he added with concern.

Autumn hid the large scrape on her arm and shook her head. "I'm fine, thanks! Let's get these guys!"

Isaac and Autumn battled the ground crew side by side. Miles came by to check on them. "Need any help?" They said they did not. The alien numbers felt manageable, and the two decided they didn't want to take valuable resources from the rest of the fight.

From Asher's position on the roof, he looked down over the lava pit. "Hey, the pit's not working. We were supposed to be farming aliens down there." He looked more closely and realized he had forgotten to activate the water candle. Asher made his way down the blue striped steps without noticing how lovingly and beautifully they had been crafted and set the candle on the altar. "Now we'll see some serious action!" He said out loud to no one. Almost instantly, the spawn rate of ground aliens increased. The aliens marched toward the candle, some with protective bubbles on their heads, others in different colored uniforms. They flocked to the candle like moths to a porch light, not noticing the pit of doom that lay between themselves and the candle. They fell one by one into the lava bucket, dropping their precious gold and armor into the pit below as Asher laughed and clapped his hands. "It's working!" he called to Miles and Owen. "We've got ourselves a real alien farm!"

Miles gave him a thumbs up and Owen murmured his approval from where he was stationed in the middle of the structure. His attention almost entirely focused on taking out gigazapper aliens, Martian engineers and the Tesla Turrets before they could inflict any damage on his friends.

The battle raged on, with the Martian saucer spewing out lasers, occasionally searing clothing and once even lighting poor Carlo's hair on fire. Sarah quickly put out the fire and promised him a fabulous haircut when the war was over. Carlo spent the rest of the battle locked in his house wailing loudly about his lovely locks. With him out of commission, Roland grew more comfortable. He whipped out his book of skulls and fired shadow-flame at any passing alien on land or in the air. Bunny was impressed with his skills and did her best to support his efforts with encouragement and the occasional confetti burst when he landed a particularly good shot.

Miles turned his focus to a nearby Scutlix and its rider. Asher joined him by his side. "Don't worry about saving the Scutlix this time. Let's just take these guys out and finish them off." Miles nodded in agreement and fired his repeater at the pair. Asher hit the Scutlix as Miles hit the rider. They high-fived happily. Just then, a laser shot between them, knocking them both back. They were both hurt. Katie the nurse and Danny the angler rushed over to help. "You're supposed to save your celebration until the end, you know," Danny scolded them.

"Reckless behavior," Katie shook her head at them as she bathed their wounds with honey. "Would have expected more from you two." She turned her attention to the burn in Miles's side and began dabbing at it angrily with a gauze pad. "Watch what you're doing. That's what I say."

"Ouch!" Miles winced in pain. "You're not being very gentle," he said accusingly.

"You're not being very careful," the nurse shot back. She placed a bandage on the wound. "There. That should hold you. Now stay out of trouble, you two," she cautioned them.

They thanked her and headed back into the battlefield where they met up with Isaac, Autumn, Hope, John, and Jack. They were all showing signs of exhaustion and none of them had escaped without any injuries. Miles's brow furrowed with concern. He, Asher, and Owen had a lot to gain from this battle, but the rest of them were just there to support them. He felt badly for roping them into such a difficult and dangerous situation. "Are you guys okay?"

"We're doing great," Autumn reassured him. "Don't worry about us. We're here to support you, no matter what."

Isaac agreed. "We've got the ground assault. You take care of what you need to do." Isaac gave Miles a gentle shove toward his position in the structure. "We're at our assigned posts, now you run along to yours and leave us to do our jobs."

Miles nodded and headed back to the safety of the structure. Had he done a terrible thing placing his friends out in the open in harm's way while he was safe indoors shooting through barriers at the ship? It may have been a good tactical move but it still wasn't fair, Miles thought. "What have I done?" he asked himself softly.

Sarah the stylist appeared at his side. "What have you done? Anything I can fix with my trusty stylish scissors?" she asked cheerfully.

"I'm afraid not," Miles replied. "I'm just feeling like all this trouble is my doing. I brought this on."

"Yeah, you did," she replied plainly. "And you'd do it again too."

Miles looked at her in surprise. "That's not very nice. You're supposed to make me feel better, not worse."

"I'm your friend. That means I'm supposed to tell you the truth. And the truth is this is all your doing, but it's also your job. Just as my job is making everyone look fabulous and Hope's job is to make those cool contraptions and Isaac's job is to tinker or something," she said gently. "Your job is to build us homes, protect us, and provide for us, isn't it?" Miles nodded. "Well, then," she continued, "taking us into a battle where we have a lot to gain is a good way to provide for us. So go out there and finish the job so we can reap the rewards!"

Miles smiled weakly. He knew she was right, though he didn't want to admit it. She'd never let him live it down if he did. "Fine. I started this, I'll finish it."

"Good," Sarah said. "But do it quickly. Everyone's looking a little tired. I don't know how much longer they can take it."

Miles looked out over his trusted crew. They were each engaged in a struggle and though the alien crowds were thinning and it looked like they might even come out of this with a win, time was running out. Miles just hoped he could pull off this battle without losing anyone in the process. He thanked Sarah, then made his way to the structure to see about taking out that spaceship.

Chapter 14:
ESCAPE FROM THE EXTRATERRESTRIALS

Miles positioned himself inside the structure, concentrating his energy on the Martian saucer. He fired his Nettle Burst through the walls as quickly as he could, knowing that taking out the saucer would reduce much of the damage his team was taking on. Suddenly, a Martian rider on a Scutlix rushed in alongside a Martian officer wearing a protective shield and a ray gunner. They seemed to have coordinated their efforts with this new attack and were focusing on taking out the structure. Pieces of the walls and ceiling were already crumbling. Miles knew his time was limited and he redoubled his efforts to take out the saucer. He wasn't sure he could take it out before the aliens destroyed the structure entirely.

Just then, Cedric wandered over with his flower of fire. "Hello. Anything I can do to help, Javier?"

Miles stifled a laugh. Even in the midst of a deadly battle, the wizard's mistakes were still funny. "How's that weapon working?"

Cedric looked at his hands as if he was surprised to find it there. "Oh, good. Good. Let me see if it works." He pointed the flower of fire up at the sky without even looking and pulled the trigger. A line of fire shot through a hole in the roof and came into contact with the saucer. It was a direct hit! The saucer burst into flame and fell out of the sky. The rain of lasers stopped. "Looks like it works just fine, eh?" Cedric grinned and walked off. "Now to see about those rabbits. I wonder where they went off to." Miles was certain he heard the wizard mumbling as he made his way through the alien attack to his house.

With the ship gone, the team was able to focus on the alien attack and come out from under cover. Jack the demolitionist ran into a herd of plain gray aliens and threw grenades right and left to take them out. "Boo yah! Take that, little gray men!" he shouted happily.

The rest of his friends began fighting with a renewed sense of spirit and purpose as well. Wrenches, fireballs, spiked balls, ranged weapons, and even Katie the nurse's poisoned knife flew at the alien enemies, dealing damage right and left. The pit around the lava bucket was filled with loot and the few remaining straggling aliens that wandered over to the water candle fell in with a plop and a hiss.

Then, just as suddenly as the battle began, it grew quiet. Everyone looked around, weapons ready to strike, but the aliens were gone.

They all let out a cheer! "Victory!" Asher shouted, grabbing Owen and Miles around the shoulders and jumping up and down.

"This calls for another party!" Bunny shouted. She activated her Party Center with a pop, and everyone was instantly wearing party hats and surrounded by balloons.

A status message appeared: "*Looks like Bunny's throwing a party!*"

Roland went up to Carlo with an outstretched hand. "Mama always said you've got to put the past behind you before you can party on."

Carlo grinned and shook his hand. "Let's paint this town red to celebrate."

"I was thinking a dark shade of pink, actually," Roland replied.

Carlo started to argue but thought better of it. "Whatever you say, my friend!"

Sarah danced by with her scissors out, popping balloons as she went. Katie put her hand on Sarah's arm. "Running with scissors is a no-no. Dancing with scissors is downright dangerous. Don't make me give you a time out in the infirmary!"

Sarah apologized and tucked her scissors away, then pulled out a pin and continued popping balloons. Katie sighed and walked away, deciding for once to let down her guard and have fun. She'd deal with all the bruises and bumps after the party was over.

Asher gathered the rest of the villagers together to start a limbo game with Cedric's magic staff. Bunny sat back and watched the fun, happy she could help her friends blow off some steam after a tough battle.

"They make great teammates, don't they?" Miles said to Owen. Owen nodded. "This is why I spend so much time in the village. I like feeling like part of something bigger, you know?"

"I understand," Owen said. "But I'm still glad we dragged you out on our adventures."

"And we brought some adventure back with us too," Miles added. "So, what's next? Are you guys going to stay here for a while?"

Owen was about to answer that he wasn't sure when Asher ran past to return to the limbo line. "Not a chance, brother! Not while there's more to conquer out there in the wide world!"

The song ended and everyone in the room heard Asher's next comment. "You should leave your village and come with us! The Three Amigos reunited together again!"

All eyes turned to Miles, some of their faces were angry, others were stunned, sad, or accusing.

Miles stood there, his mouth open but no sound escaped. He closed his eyes for a moment, wishing everyone hadn't heard Asher's request and wishing Asher hadn't made it at all.

Chapter 15:
OTHER PLANS

Miles grabbed Asher's arm and pulled him away. Owen strode after them. When they reached a quiet spot away from the crowds, Miles spun around angrily to face Asher. "Why would you say that in front of everyone like that?" he said angrily. "After everyone worked so hard to support us. Right when they're celebrating too."

"What's the big deal?" Asher asked defensively. "They're fine with us coming and going."

"For one, it makes us look ungrateful," Miles replied. "They all put a lot on the line for us. The dust hasn't even cleared and you're already running off and bringing me into your plans without asking."

"I did ask," Asher replied. "I'm asking right now."

"Just hear Asher out, okay?" Owen said gently.

"Okay," Miles replied reluctantly. "What's your next big quest?"

"Ocram," Asher and Owen said together.

Miles nodded. He had been expecting that was their goal all along and said as much to the pair.

"How did you know?" Owen asked, wide-eyed. Miles was happy to see he still had the ability to surprise his friend.

"With all three mechanical bosses defeated, Ocram is the next big boss on the list. Plus, the Soul of Blight drop is a valuable ingredient in crafting all sorts of next-generation weaponry," Miles explained. "Good luck with your quest."

"So you're not coming, then?" Asher asked. "I was expecting that from you as well."

Miles shook his head no. He was itchy to get back to his responsibilities here in the village, and he was eager to spend some time with Sarah and John. The more time they spent together, the closer they had become as friends. Plus, in the past few battles, he realized there was still so much he didn't know about this hardmode world. He had a lot more reading up to do, and all that reading could benefit Asher and Owen, along with any other warriors who came along. "My place is here for now," Miles replied simply. "But it doesn't mean I won't join you for another battle vacation again!"

Owen laughed at that comment. "We'll take you up on that, you know."

"I hope you do!" Miles replied. "I'll be reading up on the bosses you haven't faced yet so I can help."

"So you're going to be my hardmode guide after all," Owen laughed. "I knew it all along!"

"Can we make it a big announcement? I think it could help your image too," Asher asked. Miles shrugged. He knew once he told his friends he had chosen to stay that all would be forgiven anyway. He followed Asher and Owen back to the party.

As soon as they arrived, the music stopped again and everyone turned to look at them. Bunny and Sarah stared angrily, their hands on their hips. John, Jack, Isaac, and Autumn avoided their gaze. If Miles was to go on another journey, he knew those two would have asked to come. Danny looked sad. Miles realized that if he left again, Danny wouldn't get his house after all. He wanted to reassure them all right away, but he had given Asher permission to break the news so all he could do was stand and wait. Before Asher could speak, Katie confronted Miles. "Do you have an announcement to make?"

"He doesn't, but I do." Asher stepped forward. "Owen and I invited Miles to face one of our hardest enemies yet. Ocram."

John and Jack nudged each other with excitement. "He's gonna do it!" John said.

"I hope he takes us this time," Jack replied.

"Shhhh!" Autumn silenced them. "We'll miss the announcement."

"He said no," Owen announced.

"He did?" Autumn and Isaac said together, clearly surprised.

"He did!" Bunny, Sarah, and Roland called out with excitement.

Miles smiled at his friends' reaction. "I've been gone for too long already," he addressed the group. "I have new friends to build houses for," he looked at Danny who broke into a big gap-toothed grin. "And I have old friends I haven't spent enough time with in a while." Sarah blushed while John gave Miles a thumbs up. "I'm not saying I've completely hung up my weapons, but for now, my place is here."

Miles turned to Owen and Asher. "Please join me in wishing our two adventurous friends farewell and good luck!" Everyone cheered, whether it was to support Asher and Owen's quest or to express their relief that Miles was staying. "Now let's get back to the party and give these guys one heck of a send-off!"

Chapter 16:
CATCH OF THE DAY

After a good night's sleep, Asher and Owen woke before daybreak to head out on their next quest. Miles met them at the edge of the village.

"You didn't have to get up to see us off," Asher said. "But we appreciate it!"

"Actually, I got up early to tend to the farm animals," Miles replied, showing them an empty feed bucket. "I figured you guys would still be in bed."

"We wanted to get an early start. We have a lot to do," Owen chimed in.

"You know you can't summon Ocram until dark, right?" Miles asked.

"We know," Asher said sullenly. "We have to craft the suspicious looking skull first. And we need to create an arena."

"I'm happy to hear you've learned something about advance planning from our travels together!"

Miles said. "A good arena can make all the difference in battle."

"You're a good teacher, Miles," Owen said. "But don't give us any more hints. We left behind a couple of beds in your basement. If we fail, we'll wind up there and you'll greet us at breakfast one day. We'll be happy to listen to any clues you want to give us then!"

"Smart idea. I hope I see you soon walking through the gates of the village, and not appearing over pancakes after a failed battle!"

They said their farewells. Asher and Owen walked off to find adventure and Miles went to find a new adventure of his own.

He looked in on Danny who was still fast asleep in his temporary bedroom. Miles quietly gathered supplies and went off to his favorite tree to build Danny his new house. Isabella came by as Miles was setting up his workspace. "Whatcha doing?" she asked, inspecting his supplies.

"I'm building a tree house for Danny. You wouldn't want to help, would you?" Miles asked.

"I totally would. Living in a tree is one of the most perfect experiences ever. Being at one with nature and . . ."

Miles cut Isabella off. "Right, I know all about your love of nature but we have work to do. How did you get the idea to build your house in a tree in the Hallow?"

Isabella summoned a vine of protection at the base of the tree, grabbed some boards, and lifted herself up to the middle of the tree on the vine. "When you're living in the Hallow, you need a house off the ground because of the unicorns," she called down.

Miles understood completely. Those unicorns were as dangerous as they were beautiful. They could stomp a weak house flat with a person in it just by running past.

With Isabella's help and guidance, the house came together quickly and looked much better than if Miles had created it on his own. By the time Danny emerged from his house rubbing the sleep dust from his eyes, the house was finished. Danny ran up to Miles and Isabella and thanked them enthusiastically. He scrambled up the tree and flopped down in his bed. "This is the best house ever! I can see all sorts of great fishing spots from here." He scrambled back down to the ground where Miles and Isabella were smiling happily. "And that gives me an idea for a new challenge, if you're up for it, Miles."

"I'd love to," Miles replied. "I've been waiting a long time for this fishing trip, actually."

Danny turned to Isabella. "Thanks for your help in building the house, Isabella. I almost feel bad about putting that piranha tooth on your chair at the party!"

Isabella laughed. "That's okay. But I will get you back, so watch your step, little fisherman!"

"I'd like to see you try!" Danny replied.

"So, where to?" Miles asked Danny as they gathered their fishing gear.

"To the ocean," Danny replied. "Ever heard of a barking fish?" Miles shook his head no. "I haven't, either. I'm just wondering if you did!"

Miles laughed at Danny's lame attempt at humor. It was nice to be on a quest that wasn't likely to end up with a visit to the nurse or waking up in his bed after messing up.

"So what are we looking for?" Miles asked.

"I saw this bright orange and colorful fish by the ocean, and it was looking around frantically as though it was seeking a lost family member! Go catch it for me," Danny ordered.

"You mean a clownfish?" Miles asked. "That's a weird name for a fish, don't you think? They're probably not very funny," Miles observed.

"They're not," Danny answered. "But you are."

It was a long walk to the ocean, but aside from the usual passive animals and ordinary biomes, they didn't see much to note. They walked along quietly, enjoying the silence after their Martian ordeal the day before. They stopped to have a picnic on a rock at the top of a low hill. "The ocean is right down there," Danny said, pointing toward the sparkling water just a little distance away. Miles couldn't wait to get there. They quickly finished their lunch and headed to the ocean. They settled in at the shore and cast in their lines, hoping for a quick bite.

It wasn't long before Miles caught his first fish. They placed it in a bucket to bring home to their friends. "We'll have a nice feast tonight," Miles promised.

"Are you doing the cooking?" Danny asked. "I'm a great fisherman but a terrible chef!"

"We'll sharpen our cooking skills together. We have lots of time to figure it out now that I'm back home," Miles said happily.

The third fish they caught was an orange and white striped fish. It was small—too small to cook, too big to keep in the new aquarium Danny had made for him. Miles was about to throw it back before Danny stopped him.

"Clownfish!" he announced happily. "You did it. You met my challenge!"

Miles looked more closely at the fish and laughed. "I can't believe I almost threw it back!"

Danny took a hat out of his inventory and placed it on Miles's head. "Here's your prize. An Angler hat! It marks you as a true fisherman."

"Thanks!" Miles said, looking down at his reflection in the water and straightening the hat. "Let's head back to town to show our friends."

"It's early," Danny observed. "Do you want to explore a little before we head back? You never know what kinds of adventures we'll find here at the ocean."

Miles shook his head. Adventure could wait. He couldn't wait to get back home to the village and to his friends.

"I'll race you home!" he called to Danny and sprinted down the beach. Danny followed close behind. They laughed and ran all the way back home where Bunny had a party waiting for them. With good friends, every day brought a new reason to celebrate.